Dear Parent:
Your child's love of reading starts here!

Every child learns to read in a different way and at his or her own speed. Some go back and forth between reading levels and read favorite books again and again. Others read through each level in order. You can help your young reader improve and become more confident by encouraging his or her own interests and abilities. From books your child reads with you to the first books he or she reads alone, there are I Can Read Books for every stage of reading:

SHARED READING
Basic language, word repetition, and whimsical illustrations, ideal for sharing with your emergent reader

BEGINNING READING
Short sentences, familiar words, and simple concepts for children eager to read on their own

READING WITH HELP
Engaging stories, longer sentences, and language play for developing readers

READING ALONE
Complex plots, challenging vocabulary, and high-interest topics for the independent reader

ADVANCED READING
Short paragraphs, chapters, and exciting themes for the perfect bridge to chapter books

I Can Read Books have introduced children to the joy of reading since 1957. Featuring award-winning authors and illustrators and a fabulous cast of beloved characters, I Can Read Books set the standard for beginning readers.

A lifetime of discovery begins with the magical words **"I Can Read!"**

*Visit www.icanread.com for information
on enriching your child's reading experience.*

bed

pillow

crowns

pond

feathers

ponies

gift

pony

hat

scarf

ice skates

sun

icicles

trees

necklace

Ponies on Ice

by Ruth Benjamin
illustrated by Carlo Lo Raso

HarperCollins*Publishers*

It was winter in Ponyville.

 hung from the .

The  was frozen.

The  were getting

ready for the ice-skating

party.

Each  was planning

an ice dance for the party.

Triple Treat tied her .

Then she worked on flips.

Bumbleberry tied her .

Then she worked on twirls.

Kimono put on her .

Then she tried figure eights.

Pinkie Pie watched

the other  skate.

She could not do a flip.

She could not do a twirl

or a figure eight.

What would she do

on the  ?

Triple Treat saw Pinkie Pie

sitting by the .

Pinkie Pie looked sad.

"What is wrong?"

asked Triple Treat.

"I do not know any tricks,"

said Pinkie Pie.

"I will teach you tricks!"

said Triple Treat.

"Follow me!"

Pinkie Pie tied her .

The two went out

on the ice together.

Triple Treat showed

Pinkie Pie how to spin.

She showed her

how to skate backward.

She showed her how to jump.

Pinkie Pie saw the

around Triple Treat's neck.

"This is my lucky 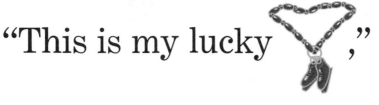,"

said Triple Treat.

"I want you to have it."

"Thank you!" said Pinkie Pie.

"I will wear it tomorrow

when I skate on the ⬤."

That night as Pinkie Pie

got into ,

she thought about the party.

She wanted to show the

what she had learned.

She put the under her .

She dreamed of .

The next day, the 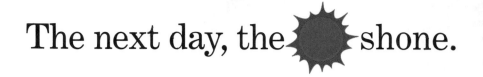 shone.

It was a good day to skate!

The  were dressed

in fancy costumes.

The costumes had sparkles,

, and 🥾. 🥾

Pinkie Pie wore the 📿.

It was time for Triple Treat

to skate.

She asked Pinkie Pie

to join her.

They skated backward.

They did spins and jumps.

The lucky sparkled.

"You are the star of the day!" the  cheered.

"Thank you!" said Pinkie Pie.

And she showed them

a fun new trick.